WHIFF, SNIFF, NIBBLE, and CHEW

The Gingerbread Boy Retold

by **Charlotte Pomerantz**

pictures by **Monica Incisa**

Greenwillow Books New York

For Ricky and Tony

Text copyright © 1984
by Charlotte Pomerantz
Illustrations copyright © 1984
by Monica Incisa
Printed in U.S.A.
First Edition
10 9 8 7 6 5 4 3 2 1

Library of Congress
Cataloging in Publication Data
Pomerantz, Charlotte.
Whiff, sniff, nibble, and chew.
Summary: A retelling in rhyme of the
adventures of the Gingerbread Boy.
[1. Stories in rhyme. 2. Folklore] I. Incisa,
Monica, ill. II. Gingerbread boy. III. Title.
PZ8.3.P564Wi 1984   398.2'1   83-14179
ISBN 0-688-02551-X
ISBN 0-688-02552-8 (lib. bdg.)

Said the little old woman
to the little old man,
"Brother, bake me a gingerbread boy,
if you can."
So the little old man
took sugar and spice,
flour and water
and everything nice.
He shaped it into
a gingerbread boy,
and the little old woman
wept tears of joy.

But soon as that gingerbread boy was done,
he jumped from the oven and started to run.

He ran till he came to a cow moo cow,
who said, "Yum-yum, come visit me now."

"Mooo," said the gingerbread boy, "toodle-oo.
I ran from home and I'll run from you."

An oink pig oink whiffed-sniffed,
"Let's play."

But the gingerbread boy squealed,
"Oink, no way.
I ran from home and a big cow big,
so I sure can run from a pig oink pig."

Said a fat cat fat,
"Come chit, come chat."

"Scat, cat. I'm a boy—not a gingerbread rat.
If I can run from home, toodle-oo,
and a pig oink pig and a moo cow moo,
I can run from a fat cat fat like you."

He ran and he ran, twenty-three skidoo,

past whiff, past sniff, past nibble, past chew.
He ran and he ran and he ran till *whew*...

His gingerbread legs
could run no more.
So he walked on home
and peeked in the door.

The little old woman jumped up with joy.
"You're home at last, my gingerbread boy!"

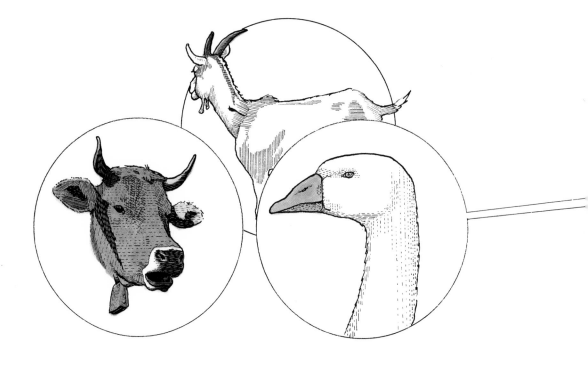

Said the little old man, with a curious grin,
"Mm, I smell gingerbread. Where you been?"
"I ran," said the gingerbread boy, "toodle-oo,
 past a pig oink pig and a moo cow moo,
 and a fat cat fat, twenty-three skidoo,
 past whiff, past sniff, past nibble, past chew.
 But I'm home to stay, if I may, with you."

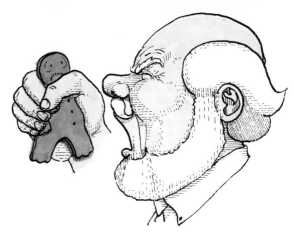

"Sure thing," said the man,
  with a wicked frown,
  and he gobbled
  that gingerbread boy right down!

The little old woman
  cried out, "You ghoul!"
"Hush, sister," he snapped, "you softheaded fool.
That cookie had no more feelings than a toy.
It just had the shape of a real live boy."

"For you, old man, he was only a snack.
For me, my gingerbread boy had come back.
He could run like the wind.
He was funny and smart.
But he knew real fear
in his gingerbread heart.

That's why he ran
from you, toodle-oo,
past the oink pig oink
and the moo cow moo,
and the fat cat fat,
twenty-three skidoo,
past whiff, past sniff,
past nibble, past chew.
But he always knew
that I loved him true,
so he came back home —
home to me, not you.
Oh! my little old woman's heart
is in pain,
for I never shall ever
shall see him again."

"Ahhh, but you shall,"
  said a voice from the deep.
"This night I shall jump
  out of him with a leap.
In his greed, he gobbled
  me down in one bite,
  so except for one toe—oh!
I'm really all right."

They waited for dark, then the two, just the two ran from the greedy old man, toodle-oo.

Past the pig oink pig and the moo cow moo,
and the fat cat fat, twenty-three skidoo.
Hand in hand, they ran the long of the night,
past whiff, past sniff, past nibble, past bite...

till they came to a man
who was little and kind,
with a gingerbread girl
who was skipping behind.

The old couple married
that night, very night
while the gingerbread children
danced round with delight.

The four built a house
against wind
and cold weather,

and when they went jogging,
they all went together.

But before they set forth,
with a small lump of dough,
the old woman patched up
the gingerbread toe.